THE PERFECT PRINCESS

Adapted by Kate Egan

Based on the Teleplay by Annie DeYoung

Based on the Story by David Morgasen and Annie DeYoung

Printed in the United States of America
First Edition 1 3 5 7 9 10 8 6 4 2
Library of Congress Control Number on file
ISBN 978-1-4231-2284-5

For more Disney Press fun, visit www.disneybooks.com
Visit DisneyChannel.com

DISNEY PRESS
New York

Carter Mason had a quiet life in a small Louisiana town. She went to school, spent time with her friends, and worked at her dad's store, Joe's Bait Shack.

Mr. Mason had another job. He was also a secret agent for the Princess Protection Program.

The P.P.P. rescued princesses from danger. It gave the girls new identities and kept them safe in hidden locations.

Carter had never met any real princesses, but she thought they cared too much about the way they looked.

Then Carter's dad brought a princess named Rosalinda home to live with them.

She was hiding from a man named General Kane, so her new name was Rosie Gonzalez.

Carter was supposed to help her blend in as a regular teenager.

It wasn't easy. Rosie wasn't used to sharing.

Carter had to tell her that they each got one side of the bedroom, not their own rooms.

She explained that nobody would serve Rosie her meals—she'd have to help herself.

One day, Carter tricked Rosie into tidying up the bait shop. Rosie spilled worms everywhere! Mr. Mason made Carter clean them up.

Rosie wasn't mad at Carter. Instead, she cooked a fancy dinner.

"To thank you for cleaning up," Rosie said.

At school, Rosie was becoming popular. A girl named Chelsea was worried that Rosie might be voted homecoming queen. Chelsea wanted the crown for herself. So she got Rosie a job at her father's frozen-yogurt shop.

Chelsea changed the setting on the frozen-yogurt machine to make Rosie look bad. Yogurt poured out and made a big mess.

Rosie didn't get upset. "I will turn the other cheek," she told Carter. "That is what princesses do."

"You're different than I thought a princess would be," Carter said later.

"It's not all about dresses and crowns," Rosie said.

Then a boy Carter liked asked Rosie out.

"A guy like him would never go out with me," said Carter.

Rosie did not agree. She thought Carter had just as much to offer as she did.

"You think being a princess is about what you wear," Rosie said. "It is about what you have to offer the world. . . . Let's find your inner princess!"

Carter had helped Rosie learn how to act like an average American girl. Now Rosie wanted to help Carter act royal. It was all about putting other people first.

The next day at school, the girls set up a table in the hallway. They hung up a sign that read, FREE TUTORING.

They helped their classmates with homework. Carter was good at math and science, and Rosie knew how to speak several languages.

Then they read to children at the local library.

Another day, the girls collected old furniture and clothes to donate and brought them to a thrift shop.

At the shop, they found some beautiful dresses. Carter tried them all on. Rosie helped her find just the right style.

"You're becoming a princess on the inside. Now you look like one, too!" Rosie said.

Then Rosie tried on some dresses. They each bought one to wear to the homecoming dance.

That night, the girls tried on their new dresses again.

Helping others had made Carter feel better about herself. The new dress didn't hurt, either.

"At home, it's my job to help people. That is what I do," Rosie explained.

"I guess I never thought about what it really means to be a princess," Carter said.

Carter finally understood what Rosie meant about being a princess on the inside—making a difference.

Then, Carter had a chance to help Rosie.

Back in Costa Luna, General Kane announced that he would marry Rosie's mother. He hoped that Rosie would come out of hiding to stop the wedding.

As soon as Rosie heard the news, she wanted to go home. Carter came up with a secret plan to help her friend. She asked Rosie to stay until the homecoming dance, and Rosie agreed.

Carter and Rosie invited girls from school to the Masons' house. Everyone got a makeover. Soon they were all acting like royalty. Rosie did not know it, but this was part of Carter's plan.

Carter also had all the girls they had helped wear masks to the dance. Carter and Rosie wore masks, too.

At homecoming, Rosie was voted queen. She gave a speech to thank her classmates.

"I've learned about friendship and loyalty and trust," she said, looking around for Carter.

Meanwhile, General Kane and his men had come to the dance to find Rosie. All the girls were wearing masks. Carter had pretended to be the princess and General Kane had captured her!

When Rosie realized what had happened, she ran after them.

Then Mr. Mason and a group of P.P.P. agents caught General Kane and his men.

"I can't believe you did all this for me!" Rosie told Carter.

"That's what princesses do, right?" Carter said.

"Yes," Rosie said, "and you truly are a princess!"

Finally, it was safe for Rosie to return to Costa Luna. Soon she was crowned queen. Mr. Mason and Carter went to the ceremony.

Carter was glad to be there with her friend. Carter knew how to look and act as if she were royalty now— and life was more fun as a princess!